This book belongs to:

For Mirren and Gowan, who always make me happy; and for Viggo, my newest reader.

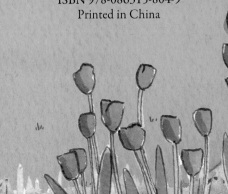

Picture Kelpies is an imprint of Floris Books
First published in 2011 by Floris Books
Text © 2011 Lari Don
Illustrations © 2011 Nicola O'Byrne
Lari Don and Nicola O'Byrne assert their right under the Copyright, Designs and
Patent Act 1988 to be identified as the Author and Illustrator of this Work. All rights
reserved. No part of this publication may be reproduced without prior permission of
Floris Books, 15 Harrison Gardens, Edinburgh www.florisbooks.co.uk
The publisher acknowledges subsidy from Creative Scotland towards the
publication of this volume.
British Library CIP Data available
ISBN 978-086315-804-9
Printed in China

How to Make a Heron Happy

Lari Don
and Nicola O'Byrne

Hamish was worried about the heron in the park.

It always looked sad and grumpy,
with its hunched-up shoulders
and long frowning eyebrows.

So one Friday, Hamish took bread crusts and biscuit crumbs to the park, in case the heron was hungry.

The ducks were happy, but the heron still looked grumpy.

So the next Friday, Hamish took a football and some friends to the park, in case the heron wanted to play.

The dogs were happy, but the heron still looked grumpy.

So the next Friday, Hamish
took some bin bags and his
family to the park to tidy
up the heron's pond.

The neighbours were happy, but the heron still looked grumpy.

So the next Friday, Hamish
took his class and some
flowers to the park to make
it look more cheerful.

The butterflies were happy, but the heron still looked grumpy.

So the next Friday, Hamish took *everyone* to the park to have a party for the heron.

Now everyone was happy.
Except the heron, who still
looked grumpy.

Hamish watched the heron
catch a fish and swallow it
in one big gulp.

"You've just had a fish for your tea,
so why do you STILL look grumpy?"
asked Hamish.

Hamish watched the heron fly wide round the
island, then settle back down in the water.
"If you weren't happy in this park, you
could just fly away," said Hamish.

Hamish watched the heron poke its beak under its wing to clean its feathers. Then he wondered, "Maybe it's not easy to smile with a hard beak. Maybe herons always look grumpy, even when they're happy!"

Hamish smiled at the heron. The heron didn't smile back.

"I think the heron is happy here," said Hamish. "And so am I."